Ruby

LOVES: Horse riding and karate lessons

HATES: Piano lessons. Snore!

WANTS V V V V MUCH: A pony and pierced ears. (But mum says I've got to wait till I'm 12!)

FAVORITE COLOUR: Pink, pink, pink!

GETS GRUMPY: When Maisie and Lulu and Fiz won't do what I tell them...

Favorite Cat

LULU

BESTEST FRIEND: Maisie. (Or Warren, my woodlouse.)

PETS: 3 cats, 12 fish, 2 guinea pigs, 4 Giant Amazonian snails, 1 rabbit, 1 rat, 1 woodlouse

WANTS V V V MUCH: A ferret!

YUKKIEST FOOD: Meat

GETS GRUMPY: When mum makes me clean out my pets' cages...

First published in Great Britain by HarperCollinsPublishers Ltd in 2000

Concept copyright © Arroyo Projects 2000
Text and characters copyright © Lindsay Camp 2000
Illustrations copyright © Daniel Postgate 2000
The author and illustrator assert the moral right to be identified
as the author and illustrator of the work.
A CIP catalogue record for this title is available from the British Library. All rights reserved.

This edition published by Barnes & Noble, Inc.,

2001 Barnes & Noble Books

ISBN 0-7607-2548-9

Printed and bound in USA
10 9 8 7 6 5 4 3 2 1

The Grumpy Little Girls and the Princess Party

Lindsay Camp and Daniel Postgate

BARNES
& NOBLE
BOOKS
NEW YORK

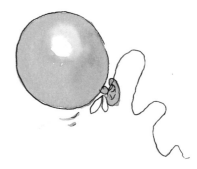

Contents

The Grumpy Little Girls and the Princess Party

Her Supreme Loveliness Princess Zelda Imelda-Mae was feeling grumpy.

It was almost her birthday and she'd commanded her Chief Lady-in-Waiting to organise a Princess Party.

"Oh Maisie," said her mum, "wouldn't you rather do something else?"

"No," said Princess Zelda Imelda-Mae. "And don't call me Maisie, or I'll have you thrown into my deepest, darkest dungeon."

"I know what," said her mum. "We could take Lulu, Ruby and Fiz to see a film, and go for a pizza afterwards."

"Princesses hate pizza," said Princess Zelda Imelda-Mae. "I want a Princess Party, and that's that."

"Hmm," said her mum. "I'll have to ask the King what he thinks about it."

Next day, before school, Maisie handed out the invitations.

Lulu and Ruby were very excited, but Fiz was a bit grumpy.

"I hate dressing up," she panted, skipping hard.

"It's OK," said Maisie, who was in a good mood. "I don't mind if you come in your dungarees."

"As long as you wear a crown," said Ruby, firmly.

By order of
Her Supreme Loveliness
Princess Zelda Imelda-Mae,
you are commanded to attend
a Princess Party.

On the day of the party, Maisie woke up very early indeed. She put on her long sparkly princess dress straight away.

"Is it nearly half past three?" she asked, for the fifth time, just after breakfast.

"Not quite yet, Your Fabulous Gorgeousness," replied her dad.

"Oh, I can't wait for my Princess Party," sighed Maisie.

At last the doorbell rang, and there was Lulu – who arrived first because she only lived next door. Maisie gasped. She'd never seen Lulu looking so... princess-ish.

"Greetings, Princess Zelda Imelda-Mae," said Princess Lulu, handing over her present.

And after that, the doorbell kept ringing, and more and more princesses arrived, all looking very beautiful – even Princess Fiz, who was wearing a shiny silver tutu over her dungarees.

But for some reason, Maisie found she wasn't really enjoying herself. There was something not quite right about this Princess Party...

"Let's start the games," said Maisie's dad.

"But Ruby isn't here yet," said Lulu.

Just then, the doorbell rang once more, and into the room swept Princess Ruby.

Everybody stopped what they were doing and stared. Ruby's mum made costumes for TV programmes, and the princess dress she'd made for Ruby was absolutely brilliant.

It was all shimmery, and there were millions of jewels – rubies, of course – sewn all over it. A long floaty bit trailed along the ground.

Ruby did a twirl, and everyone started to clap!

Everyone except Maisie – who ran out of the room and up the stairs, screaming, "It's not fair! It's my party and I want to be the most beautiful princess!"

"Oh dear," said Maisie's dad, following her.

"Who wants to play Musical Thrones?" asked Maisie's mum.

Upstairs, Maisie slammed her bedroom door behind her. Her dad knocked gently.

"Excuse me, Your Utter Beautifulness, your loyal subjects are awaiting your majestic presence downstairs."

"Go away, not playing, stupid game!" shouted Maisie.

"All right, Maisie," said her dad. "You can come down when you've stopped being so silly."

Maisie knew she had been silly, very silly to have a Princess Party. She should have had a Servants and Slaves Party, and then she would have been the only princess.

She lay on her bed, listening to the others shouting and laughing downstairs and feeling very grumpy indeed... until suddenly, she heard a scream.

It sounded like Lulu.

Maisie crept to the top of the stairs to see what was the matter. It **was** Lulu, holding something small in her hand, and howling.

"What happened?" asked Maisie, coming downstairs.

"Fiz killed Warren!" wailed Lulu.

Fiz was looking miserable, too. And she'd gone bright red.

"It was an accident," explained Maisie's mum. "Fiz was bouncing on the sofa, and she landed on the matchbox with Lulu's pet woodlouse in it."

"He's completely squashed!" sobbed Lulu.

"Poor Warren," said Maisie, forgetting her own grumpiness.

And then she had a good idea.
"Come upstairs with me, everyone,"
she said. "We need to get changed."

"This isn't a Princess Party any more," explained Maisie. "It's a Burying Warren Party. We're going to bury him in the garden."

And so they did.

With Lulu behind her, carrying the squashed matchbox, Maisie led everyone out into the garden.

"What do we do now?" said Ruby, who was rather grumpy about having to take off her beautiful princess dress.

"Shhh!" said Maisie. "I'm going to say a poem..."

"O Warren," she began, "you were wonderful,

And you belonged to Lulu.

But now that you've been squashed by Fiz,

I'm sure we're going to miss you."

Then they all sang a sad song that they had learned at school about an old donkey, because they didn't know any songs about woodlice.

Very carefully, Fiz dug a little hole and Lulu put the matchbox into it, and covered it with soil.

"We need a stone to put on top," said Maisie. "So we'll remember where he is."

"What about this one?" said Fiz, picking up a huge rock.

"Oh look!" said Ruby, pointing.

Under where the rock had been, was the most enormous woodlouse.

L ulu's eyes lit up. "Oh, please can I have him?
Please, please, please!"

"Of course you can," said Maisie's mum.

"I'll find a matchbox for him."

"You can put him in your party bag," suggested Maisie, wondering why...

...she hadn't thought of a Burying Warren Party in the first place.

The
Grumpy Little Girls
and the
Wobbly Sleepover

Lulu was staying the night at Maisie's.
They lived next door to each other and had been best friends since they were babies, so they often stayed over with each other.

Lulu had brought Alvin with her.

After their bath, they played Circus Ladies, and taught Alvin to do all kinds of tricks.

At bedtime, when Maisie's mum came up to say goodnight, the girls were whispering together.

"What is it?" she asked.

"What are you two planning now?"

"We were wondering... " said Lulu, a bit shyly.

" ...if we could have a sleepover?" finished Maisie.

"Isn't this a sleepover?" asked Maisie's mum.

"No, silly," said Maisie. "A proper real one – with popcorn, and videos and lots of people."

"Hm," said Maisie's mum doubtfully. "I'm not sure. I'll have to talk to dad about it."

Maisie was rather grumpy after her mum went downstairs,
because "talking to dad" nearly always meant no.

"Never mind," said Lulu. "We'll ask my mum and dad in the morning."

So they did.

But Lulu's mum and dad said no straight away.

"Maybe one day," said Lulu's mum.

"Nobody would get a wink of sleep," said Lulu's dad.

"It's not fair!" complained Lulu and Maisie together, very grumpily indeed.

But just then, something happened that made Lulu cheer up. Something inside her mouth. Wriggling her tongue around, she noticed something – well, loose.

"Hey," she shouted. "I've got a wobbly tooth!"

She poked it with her finger. There was no doubt about it, it was her very first wobbly tooth.

"Come and see," she said to Maisie.
"You can wobble it if you like."
But Maisie didn't want to.

"I think wobbly teeth are silly," she said. "Come on, let's ring up Ruby and see if her mum will let us have a sleepover."

Ruby was very excited when she answered the phone. "You'll never guess what!" she said. "I've got a wobbly tooth!"

"So have I!" said Lulu.

"Ask her about the sleepover,"
hissed Maisie, crossly.

Ruby's mum said no, too.

B ut on Monday at school, when Lulu and Ruby had shown each
other their wobbly teeth, they told Fiz about the sleepover.
And she said they could definitely have one at her house.

Fiz had three very big brothers, and her house was always full of teenagers in sleeping bags. So she was sure her mum and dad wouldn't mind at all.

And she was right. They said it would be absolutely fine, and that they could have the sleepover next Saturday night.

The girls were very excited.

"I bet my wobbly tooth will have fallen out by then," said Lulu.

"I bet mine will come out before yours," said Ruby.

"Hey," said Maisie, with her finger in her mouth. "I think one of my teeth is just a tiny bit wobbly..."

After that, the Great Wobbly Tooth Race began. Whenever Lulu, Ruby or Maisie didn't have anything else to do with their fingers, they wobbled furiously.

Only Fiz didn't join in. She was too busy learning to skip backwards.

At last, the day of the sleepover arrived. In the car on the way to Fiz's house, Lulu and Maisie were still wobbling away.

"I bet Ruby's tooth has come out," said Lulu. "She said she was going to tie a piece of string round it, and then tie the string to a door handle, and slam the door."

"That's cheating!" said Maisie.

But when they arrived, they found Ruby's tooth still hanging on to Ruby's gum. Soon, they all forgot about their teeth and started to enjoy their sleepover.

They had pizza.

They ate popcorn
and watched two videos.

They made a pile of mattresses on the playroom floor, and bounced on them.

And, of course, they had a pillow fight.

Then Maisie made up a pop group, called Maisie-May and the
Amazing Singing Women – and taught the others how to do a
special dance, behind her.

After that, Fiz's dad said it was very late and time for them to get some sleep! So the girls wriggled into their sleeping bags.

But they didn't go to sleep.

Maisie told a very scary ghost story, and Fiz made horrible noises to go with it. Lulu started playing with Alvin, who had come with her in her overnight bag.

Only Ruby snuggled down quietly. She had some serious wobbling to get on with. In fact, she was quite sure she was just a few more wobbles from winning the race...

"Hey!" shouted Maisie, noticing what she was doing. "Ruby's wobbling!"

Immediately, Maisie and Lulu stopped what they were doing and started wobbling, too.

Alvin saw his chance to escape. Leaping off Lulu's lap, he shot across the room, and scurried up to the very top of the curtain.

"Don't worry," said Fiz. "I'll climb up the bookcase and get him."

Wobble, wobble, wobble went Lulu, Maisie and Ruby.

"I can nearly reach him," said Fiz from the top of the bookcase.

Wobble, wobble, wobble...

"If I just lean over like this, and—"

Crash! went Fiz.

The others stopped wobbling, and rushed over to her.

"Are you all right?" gasped Ruby.

"I think so," said Fiz calmly, picking herself up. "I banged my mouth. It feels a bit funny, but it doesn't hurt too much." And she smiled bravely.

The
Grumpy Little Girls
and the
Bouncy Ferret

There was one thing Lulu wanted
more than anything else in all the world.
She already had 1 rat, 1 rabbit, 2 guinea pigs, 3 cats,
4 Giant Amazonian snails and 12 fish.
Oh yes, and a woodlouse called Warren.

Now she was desperate for a ferret. But she knew what her mum and dad would say.

Her mum would say, "You've got enough animals already."

And her dad would say, "You don't look after them properly. How long is it since you cleaned out that poor rabbit's hutch?"

So on Saturday morning, Lulu cleaned out Rex's hutch.

Then, at lunchtime, she said to her mum and dad, very quickly, "Can I have a ferret? It's ages since I had any new animals."

"You don't look after the ones you've got," said her dad. "How long is it since you cleaned out Rex's—"

"This morning," Lulu cut him off. "I cleaned out Rex's hutch this morning."

Her mum and dad looked at each other.

"Aren't ferrets rather fierce and bitey?" asked her mum.

"No," said Lulu. "I saw one on TV and it slept in the man's bed, under his pillow. So can I? Please, please, please!"

"No!" said her mum and dad, together.

And then her mum said, more kindly,
"Maybe for your birthday, Lulu. But not now.
A ferret would be much too expensive."

But it was years and years until Lulu's birthday,
and she wanted a ferret now.

"It's not fair!" she said, very grumpily indeed.

She was still quite grumpy after lunch when her dad offered to take her to the park, where there was an excellent new climbing frame.

But she cheered up when they arrived and found Maisie and Ruby already playing on it.

"It's a spaceship," explained Maisie. "And those are evil aliens who aren't allowed to come on board," she went on, pointing to some little boys.

When they got tired of that game, they sat on the grass in the sunshine, and Lulu told Maisie and Ruby about how much she wanted a ferret, and how her mum and dad said it was too expensive.

"You could save up," said Ruby.

"But I only get 50p a week," groaned Lulu. "It would take ages."

"I know what we could do," said Maisie, who didn't like to see her best friend looking miserable. "We could steal lots of money from a bank. We'd need a big sack to put all the money in, and masks to cover up our faces."

L ulu laughed.

"I think that's a silly idea," said Ruby. "How would we get to
the bank, anyway? We'd have to ask one of our mums to take us...

...and then they'd want to know why, and we'd get into trouble."

Maisie looked grumpy. "I bet you can't think of a better idea," she said.

"I can," said Ruby. "We could open a shop, and sell things that we make."

Lulu and Maisie stared at her with their mouths open. It wasn't a good idea. It was a brilliant one.

"Come on," said Lulu excitedly. "Let's go back to my house, so we can start our shop straight away."

But when they got back to Lulu's house, the shop didn't seem quite such a brilliant idea after all.

To start with, they couldn't agree what to call it. Ruby said she'd thought of it, so it should be called Ruby's Superstore.

But Lulu and Maisie didn't like that name.

Then they argued about what the shop should sell. So, in the end, they had to open three shops.

Lulu lived in a quiet road, so they didn't have many customers. In fact, they didn't have any except Lulu's mum, who bought something from each shop. After a while, they got bored.

"We're never going to get enough money for a ferret like this," wailed Lulu.

Just then, Lulu's mum called out, "Lulu, Fiz is on the phone!"

Fiz sounded very excited, and rather out of breath.

"You'll never guess what I'm doing," she panted.

"What?" said Lulu.

"Not telling," gasped Fiz. "You'll have to come and see."

So Lulu's dad gave the girls a lift to Fiz's house.
And there in the garden, they saw it.

"It's fantastic!" said Ruby.

"It's totally wicked," said Fiz, whose big brothers were always saying that kind of thing. "I could go on bouncing all day. But you can have a go."

Ruby and Maisie each had a turn on the trampoline. Lulu watched them, feeling rather miserable about her ferret.

"Go on, Lulu," said Maisie, climbing off. "It's brilliant!"

So Lulu climbed on to the trampoline and started to bounce, quite little bounces to begin with, then higher and higher ones.

And as she bounced, she started to feel better – as if, well, as if everything was going to be all right.

At bedtime, Lulu said to her mum, "Mum, remember when you went on that long walk, and everybody gave you lots of money?"

"Yes," said her mum. "My sponsored walk."

"Does it have to be a walk?" asked Lulu. "Could it be a sponsored something else?"

"I suppose it could," said Mum, looking puzzled. "As long as the money went to a good cause."

"Oh yes, it will," said Lulu.

"What are you planning?"

"Nothing, Mum," said Lulu, closing her eyes.

But two weeks later, on a sunny Saturday, Lulu, Maisie, Ruby and Fiz held their Grand Sponsored Bounce.

Each of them was going to bounce in turns, until they'd bounced all morning.

Half the money, the girls had agreed with their parents, was going to the RSPCA, to help look after sick and lost animals.

The other half? Well, Lulu's mum and dad had a pretty good idea...

...how Lulu was planning to spend it.

The
Grumpy Little Girls
and the
Naughty Little Boy

"Oh, Fiz, don't make such a fuss," said her mum. "It's only for a few days."

"I don't care," shouted Fiz, from near the top of the tallest tree in the garden. "I hate him and I'm not going to play with him."

"He's not so bad," said Fiz's mum. "And anyway, he may have changed. It's ages since you last saw him."

Just then, the front doorbell rang. "That'll be them now."

"Don't care," said Fiz, very grumpily indeed. "Not coming down."

Fiz's cousin Archie was coming to stay, with his mum.

Fiz liked her auntie, whose name was Elaine. But Archie –

well, Archie was only little but he was BIG trouble...

"Bang, bang, bang...BLAP...BOOOOOM!!!"

yelled Archie, pointing his spoon at Fiz.

It was just after lunch, and Fiz and Archie were in the garden,

where they'd had their pudding.

"Fiz dead," shouted Archie. "Fiz lie down!"

"No," said Fiz.

Archie stirred the spoon round and round in his melted ice cream.

Then he flicked the spoon as hard as he could towards Fiz.

"Splash!" he shouted, happily, flicking his spoon again.

Fiz sighed. This was even worse than she'd thought. Archie had already broken the heads off two of her Astropets, thrown her new skipping rope down the loo, and pulled all the tape out of her favourite Yig and Yogg video.

Just then, one of Fiz's big brothers came into the garden. Maybe he'd help her deal with Archie.

"Hey, Fiz. Hey, Archie," he said. "Seen my skateboard?"

"Boom, BLAT, CHAGGA, CHAGGA, CHAGGA," bellowed Archie. "Joel dead."

"Cool," muttered Joel, disappearing inside.

It was no good, thought Fiz. She'd have to escape. While Archie was busy stamping on some ants, she started climbing the tree again, as quickly as she could.

Meanwhile, not far away, Maisie was having trouble with a little boy, too. A very little boy.

She was playing with The Blob. At least, she was trying to.

They were in a rowing boat, surrounded by hungry sharks. But The Blob, whose real name was Sebastian, kept crawling out of the boat and into the sea.

"Stupid Blob," growled Maisie, grumpily. "Now the sharks have eaten you!"

Fiz was nearly half way up the tree before Archie noticed. "Fiz come down!" he shouted.

But she just went on climbing.

Archie looked at the tree thoughtfully. "Archie climb," he announced, marching towards it.

Oh no, thought Fiz. It was quite a difficult tree, so he'd be sure to fall down and hurt himself. Or he'd get stuck and they'd have to call the Fire Brigade...

"It's all right, Archie, I'm coming down," she called, miserably.

Suddenly, Fiz had a good idea. Of course! She'd ask Ruby round to help her. Everyone always did what Ruby told them...

Everyone except Archie.

He **bit** Ruby.

Ruby pointed her finger at Archie and told him to play quietly in the sandpit, and he just leant forward and snapped his teeth together. Ruby screamed so loudly that Fiz's mum and Elaine came rushing out.

"I am sorry," said Elaine, when she saw the bite marks.

"I'm afraid he does that sometimes."

At Maisie's house, The Blob was still causing problems. He was supposed to be helping the Most Famous Chef in the World to prepare a feast for six princesses.

But he just kept on knocking things over, and drinking all the champagne.

"Oh Blob," sighed Maisie, "you're hopeless at pretending!"

For a little while after biting Ruby, Archie was good. But only a very little while. Soon, he was charging round the garden knocking the tops off flowers with a long piece of bamboo, and growling at the girls when they tried to stop him.

Fiz and Ruby looked at each other. "Maybe Lulu would know what to do," said Fiz.

So they rang Lulu, and asked her to come and play. They didn't say anything about Archie.

Lulu arrived a little later with an interesting-shaped lump in her sweatshirt.

"Show Alvin to Archie," said Fiz, thinking that might calm him down a bit.

Lulu pulled out a large brown rat.

"Archie hold mouse," said Archie.

"He's a rat, silly," said Lulu, putting Alvin on her shoulder.

"And I don't think you'd better hold him. He sometimes bites."

"So does Archie," said Ruby, showing her poor finger to Lulu.

Archie saw his chance. He reached up, grabbed Alvin and raced off towards the house with him.

"Quick!" shouted Lulu. "We've got to rescue Alvin." And the girls started chasing Archie round the garden.

Luckily, Archie thought this was such a good game that he lost interest in Alvin, who wriggled out of his fat little hands. Lulu quickly scooped Alvin up and tucked him safely back inside her sweatshirt.

The girls collapsed, exhausted, on the lawn. Archie jumped up and down, shouting, "Chase Archie! Chase Archie!"

"What are we going to do?" said Fiz.

"I know," said Ruby. "We could lock him in the shed."

"I don't think that would be very kind," said Fiz.

"Or we could get a very long roll of sticky tape and stick him to the tree," said Lulu, who was still upset about Alvin's narrow escape.

"I suppose we could ask Maisie to come and help," said Fiz, doubtfully. "She might know what to do with him."

But do you think she did?

Well, yes. When Maisie arrived a little later, she knew exactly what to do with Archie. She took one look at him and said, "Oh, what a darling baby gorilla."

Everybody looked at Archie. For a moment, Archie looked at Maisie. Then he swung his arms low down to the ground, and started making soft hoo-hoo-hoo noises.

"Archie griller," he grunted.

"Come on," said Maisie to the others. "Pretend we're filming ladies with television cameras, and the baby gorilla is hiding in that bush over there."

As soon as he heard this, Archie went and hid in the bush.

When the girls got tired of that game, they were Strict Teachers and Archie was a very well-behaved little boy who'd just started at their school.

And after that, they were Kind Mummy Dinosaurs and he was a newborn stegosaurus who was so tiny he couldn't walk or make any noise yet...

At teatime, Fiz's mum and Elaine came into the garden.

"Oh, doesn't he look adorable," said Fiz's mum.

"I hope he hasn't been a nuisance," said Elaine.

Fiz and Ruby looked at each other.

"No, he's been a brilliant little stegosaurus," said Maisie,
wondering if she might be able to swap The Blob for Archie.

Maisie

BESTEST FRIEND: Lulu

PETS: Only the Blob – (my baby brother!)

FAVORITE GAME: Let's Pretend!

YUMMIEST FOOD: Slimy worms (Spaghetti, silly!)

SCARIEST SCARY THING: Spiders. Eeeek!

GETS GRUMPY: When Lulu won't play Let's Pretend...

FIZ

REAL NAME: Felicity. Yurgh!

BESTEST THING: Bouncing on my trampoline

WANTS V V V V MUCH: To learn to do a proper cartwheel

HATES: Playing quietly indoors

GETS GRUMPY: When my big brothers sit on me...